RUSH HOUR

Christine Loomis • illustrations by Mari Takabayashi

HOUGHTON MIFFLIN COMPANY

BOSTON • 1996

Text copyright © 1996 by Christine Loomis
Illustrations copyright © 1996 by Mari Takabayashi

All rights reserved. For information about permission to reproduce
selections from this book, write to Permissions, Houghton Mifflin Company,
215 Park Avenue South, New York, New York 10003.

For information about this and other Houghton Mifflin
trade and reference books and multimedia products, visit
The Bookstore at Houghton Mifflin on the World Wide Web
at http://www.hmco.com/trade/.

Manufactured in the United States of America

Book design by David Saylor
The text of this book is set in 19-point Martin Gothic Medium.
The illustrations are watercolor, reproduced in full color.

HOR 10 9 8 7 6 5 4 3 2 1

LIBRARY OF CONGRESS CATALOGING-IN-PUBLICATION DATA
Loomis, Christine.
Rush hour / by Christine Loomis ;
illustrations by Mari Takabayashi.   p.   cm.
Summary: Describes the hustle and bustle as people rush to work in
the morning and home again at night, taking trolleys, subways,
bikes, ferries, vans, and more.
ISBN 0-395-69129-X
[1. Vehicles—Fiction.   2. Traffic congestion—Fiction.
3. Stories in rhyme.]   I. Takabayashi, Mari, ill.
II. Title.   PZ8.3.L8619Ru   1996
[E]—dc20   94-47192   CIP   AC

For Hutch, whose love and enthusiasm
for things with wheels is awesome
—C. I.

For my mother in Tokyo
and for the memory of my father
—M. T.

Alarms are buzzing,
Day is dawning,

Sleepy people
Wake up yawning.

Showers splash,

Teeth are brushed,

Hair is combed,

Breakfast rushed.

Out their doors
Go moms and dads,
Lugging tools
Or books and pads.

Some alone,
Some with strollers,
Walkers, runners,
Readers, rollers,

Running, jumping
Onto trains,

Subways,

buses,

Boats,

and planes,

Taxis,

bikes,

A car-pool van,

Cars of blue and red and tan.

Engines start up with a jerk.
People hurry off to work.

Horns go beep-beep, whistles blow,

Planes go fast,

Trucks go slow.

Trolleys sway,

Ferries rock,

Time keeps ticking
On the clock.

Cars on side streets,
Trains on tracks,
Whizzing,
Zipping,
Clicky Clack,

Rumbling,
Roaring,
Jiggling,
Jumping,
Left turn,
Right turn,
Backing,
Bumping.

Through the tunnels,
On the highways,

Over bridges,
Roads, and byways,

Down the river,

In the air,

People rushing everywhere!

In a blink
They disappear.
Trains are empty,

Tunnels clear.

Streets are quiet,
No more mobs.

People have begun their jobs.

When day is over,
Each job ends.

Workers wave
Good-bye to friends.

Then they race
To catch the trains,

Subways,

buses,

Boats,

and planes,

Taxis,  bikes,

A car-pool van,

Cars of blue and red and tan.

Down the river,
Underground,
Traffic creeping
Homeward bound.

Over bridges,
Roads, and byways,
Through the tunnels,
On the highways,

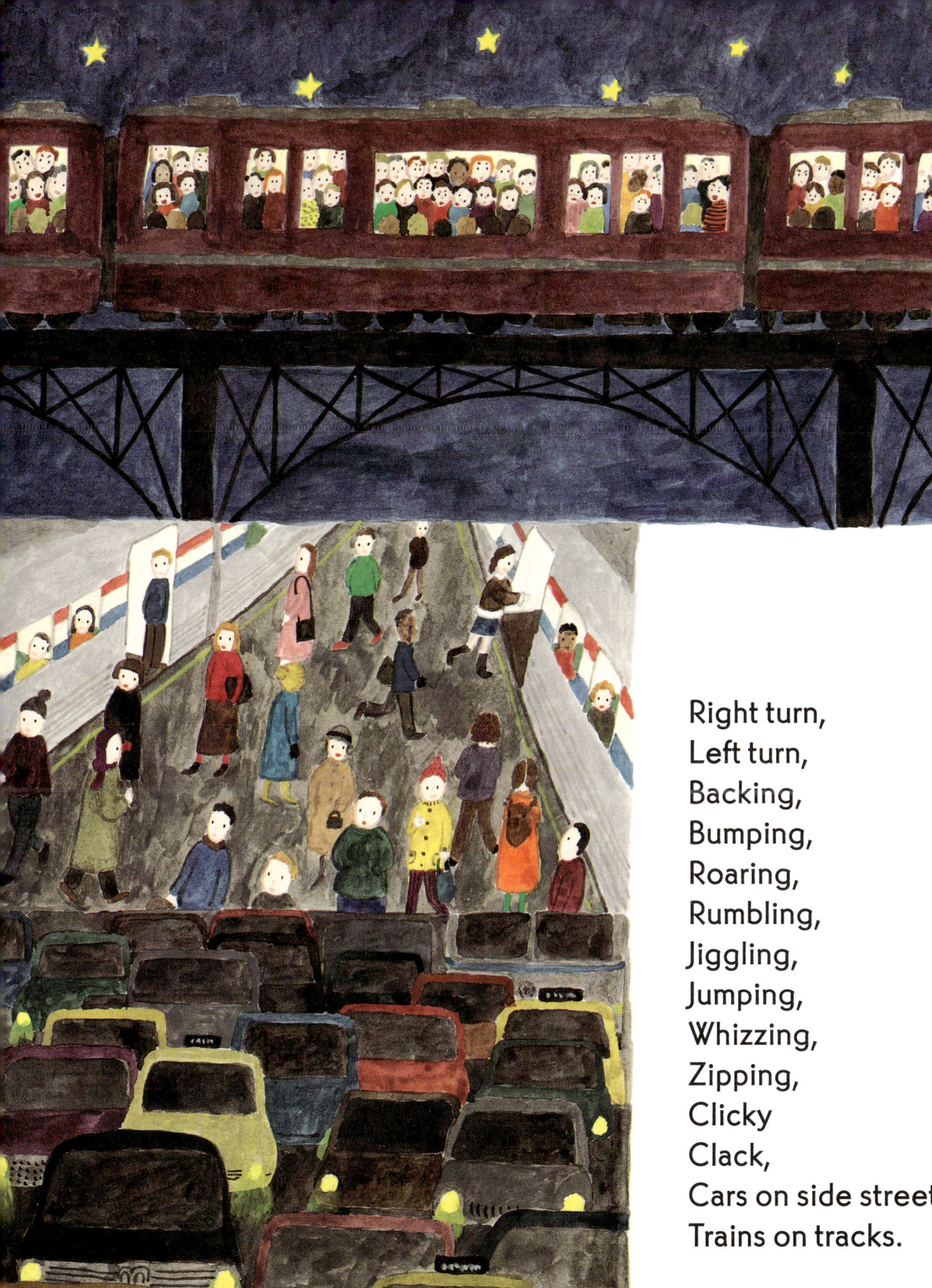

Right turn,
Left turn,
Backing,
Bumping,
Roaring,
Rumbling,
Jiggling,
Jumping,
Whizzing,
Zipping,
Clicky
Clack,
Cars on side streets,
Trains on tracks.

Horns go beep-beep,
Whistles blow.

Nighttime lights
Begin to glow.

Doors swing open.
Kids run fast.

Moms and dads
Are home at last.

Monroeton Public Library
Monroeton, Pa. 18832